Chicken Nuggets

Chicken Nuggets
First Edition
Copyright © 2014 Robert Tyson.
ISBN 978-1-941347-00-3

Photos and sketches Copyright © 2014 by Robert Tyson

Grace Garland Publishing
P.O. Box 68
Winston, GA 30187
www.GraceGarlandPublishing.com

Ordering Information:
Quantity sales. Special discounts are available on quantity purchases by corporations, associations, and others. For details, contact the publisher at the address above.

Printed in the United States of America

To My Mom and Dad –
And my friend Roy

Contents

Acknowledgements

The person I want to thank most for this book is my wife, Lynn. Despite having listened to these stories for 35 years, she still endured the countless reading and editing sessions. She contributed ideas and kept us focused on what we were trying to accomplish. She also inspired me to take on the sketches, which I thought were way beyond my skills. Most of all, I want to thank her because her confidence in me never wavers.

I would also like to thank my children, Matt and Karlyn, for their encouragement, ideas – and honest feedback. They have heard these stories all their lives and still have the enthusiasm to endure another re-telling in print.

In addition, I'd like to thank our editor, Stephanie, whose reviews, corrections, and insights were a great contribution and helped to finalize the book.

Gettin' Started

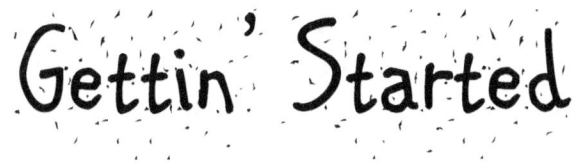

Growing up rural Georgia in the sixties, I did not know how bad or how good I had it. As a kid, I just lived there and thought other kids lived much the same as me. There were a few differences, but I really did not think much about it at the time.

After having a few years to mull it over, and what with hindsight being 20/20 and all, I realized that I *might* have had a few unique experiences. Before my memory fades, I thought it would be good to share a few of them.

Now, I am not saying that all these stories are true and factual, but there is some element of reality in all of them. Names were changed to protect both the innocent and the guilty. I thought that was a nice thing to do. If anyone in these stories told their own version, I would want them to change my name too. Treat others as you want to be treated – as the good book says.

That's about as much religion as you'll get out of these stories.

You're not going to hear much about politics either. I don't care much for politicians. However, if I ever ran for office, I do have a platform on which I'd base my whole campaign – the introduction of a National Fishing License or "NFL". A fishing license that would let you fish in any state! With all the anglers on my side, I could probably run for president!

I recently read that every time you open a memory, the memory changes. It has something to do with the wiring of your brain and how it tries to fill in the gaps and make connections where there are none.

Now, I don't know about all that. I do know that if I tell a story and fill in a few gaps, that it's a much better story. So before I completely corrupt all my memories by thinking about them, I thought it best to write them down.

Little things like scraping red clay off your boots, drinking a cold glass of sweet tea after hauling hay, smelling the musty sweat of a horse after a hard ride, or lying in the grass looking at the clouds – they all add up to some sweet memories that I don't want to lose.

Don't misunderstand, I've shed my share of tears and had my fill of fears but many of those moments have faded away into the background. Maybe it's because I don't open those memories as much so the gaps never get filled in.

I really hope you enjoy these stories. Not much preaching, not much politics – just a few simple stories of growing up in the South.

Chicken Nuggets

My Mama made the best-fried chicken. That's not just my family talking but everyone who's ever tasted it agrees. It was golden-brown, crispy with just the right amount of crust, and succulent white meat. Succulent – I don't use that word often. It never sounds right if you're conversing out loud, but it is absolutely the right word for that chicken!

I've eaten fried chicken high and low, near and far, restaurants to gas stations, back yard fryers to pot luck dinners and I stand by my original statement – nobody made fried chicken as good as my Mama. Running a close second was Aunt Martha – she could fry anything!

One particular Sunday, my mom and dad took us to eat dinner with Aunt Martha, Uncle Jack, and their family. To this day, I'm not certain where they fit into the overall family structure. I never heard either of my parents claim them.

For the trip, my dad piled two adults and five kids into a 1950 model Ford. My dad really liked those '50 Fords. He had about five of them in various states of repair, or disrepair, depending on how you looked at it. He always said it took five cars just to keep two running.

Between Aunt Martha and Uncle Jack's brood and our group of seven, we filled every space around the table. I had a spot that was barely wide enough to put my plate. I was shoulder to shoulder so tightly between two cousins that I felt I was in a cocoon. That didn't matter. We were eagerly anticipating the upcoming meal – fresh cut corn, mashed potatoes, hot biscuits, and big glasses of ice-cold, sugar-sweet tea.

Everything stretched out before us family-style, farther than the hand could reach. In the middle was the main course, a huge platter of fresh from the pan, sizzlin' fried chicken. We all commented that it was the prettiest platter of chicken we had ever seen. Fried to a crispy golden brown, the steam floated across the table and tickled our nostrils – a heavenly aroma with a perfect presentation.

We had to exhibit self-control until the blessing was over. Never seen without her Bible, Aunt Martha was the most church-going member of the family, so naturally, she said the blessing. She had a way of mixing the Lord's words with the practicality of everyday life.

Aunt Martha cleared her throat and bowed her head. The room immediately went silent as each person followed suit. Then, in her raspy and fervent voice, she began the blessing.

"Lord, thank you for bringing us all together for this Sunday dinner, and please watch over Cousin Lucky when he returns to the County Farm tomorrow.

"We also want to thank you for that joyous wedding last month between Uncle Harry and Cousin Mary. It was wonderful to see both sides of the family together again.

"We're so grateful for all you've done for us. We even owe you a special thanks for today's meal. You knew we were a mite shy of chicken for today's dinner so you sent that possum our way last week. It certainly helped to fill up the platter! Once again, we thank you. In God's name we pray, Amen."

About three seconds after the "Amen," the magnitude of Aunt Martha's words settled on everyone. You could read the faces like a book and they all said the same thing – "Possums don't have wings."

That realization generated a sudden mad rush of hands towards the fried chicken platter. Everyone was fending for himself or herself. Tea was spilling as people jumped up from the table trying to grab a real piece of chicken. With one or two exceptions, no one wanted the fried possum substitute.

That's what started this chicken riot – everyone reaching and grabbing, maneuvering for a wing. Wings were split apart as hands fought over them. All I pulled back was the third joint of a wing, the one that looks like it has hair on it.

Fried chicken will do that to you. When you gotta have it, you gotta have it and a possum is not a reasonable substitute.

"Save me a possum foot! I like the crispy ones!" That was Uncle Jack yelling from the end of the table. He was a real possum connoisseur but slow at jumping up from the table.

Aunt Martha just sat back and smiled. "My, everyone sure seems to like my fried chicken today."

That, and no one wanted to eat a possum.

When the crumbs settled, the only pieces that were left on the platter was anything that resembled a thigh. By his own wish, Uncle Jack had all four possum feet.

"When you kill a possum, you have to clean and dress it quick or it'll sneak away from you. Even then, you have to keep a close watch on him until he's fully cooked." Uncle Jack was the most knowledgeable person on possums that I knew.

Let's face it, chickens (real chickens, not camouflaged possums) were made to be Sunday dinner. It is a special quality that chickens have. After feeding and raising one for months and sometimes years, it is hardly a second thought to go out, chop off its head, pluck its feathers, and flop it down on the table. You never even name a chicken.

Very few animals can generate that sort of indifference.

We fattened up a good fryer for a couple of weeks before the planned meal. We usually kept a chicken in preparation at all times. There was a smaller pen where we kept these chickens and they ate like kings for those two weeks!

"Son, you better feed the chickens a little extra corn for the next few days. I got my eye on that white one." My dad pointed toward dirty, white rooster. As a chicken, you really did not want my dad to have his eye on you.

"We all have our eye on that white one, Dad." I almost stumbled on my words from watching the chicken too closely.

My dad sort of chuckled. The white rooster was a real menace. It was the last survivor of a bunch of Easter chickens that I bought.

Easter chickens were baby chicks dipped in food coloring. They looked like little Easter eggs with legs. They were red, pink, blue, and yellow. After Easter, the man at the Dime Store let me buy them all for five cents each. I bought him out for two dollars. They all turned out to be roosters.

Through mostly natural calamities, like being eaten by a fox, hit by a car, or eaten on Sunday; the forty chicks were gradually weeded down to eighteen strong roosters.

They were a real nuisance to the hens. Mostly they just chased them around. The hens did a lot of squawking and flapping but figured out pretty quickly that they could just fly up and roost in the lower branches of the trees. The bigger roosters just did not have enough power to reach them.

Since they couldn't fly, these strapping young roosters got bored with the hens and they started on the dogs. The puppies were first. I don't think they really wanted to have a carnal encounter with the dogs. It wasn't entirely ruled out, but no one dared to mention the subject. We just assumed they were crazy chickens.

Every time the roosters saw one of the puppies, they attacked it, jumped on their backs, pecked their necks, and scratched them with their spurs.

The puppies learned to stay under the cars so the chickens could not get to them. This started the roosters on the bigger dogs and then the cats. These bigger animals soon started living under the cars, too.

The chickens reigned in terror wherever they went. We even started calling them "The Roosters" since they were more like a gang than chickens.

When The Roosters could no longer get to the smaller creatures, they started on us.

They had quite an approach. First, they teased you. They walked boldly up to you, looked you straight in the eye with one of their tiny red eyes, and then dropped one of their wings and walked sideways towards you while fluttering that wing just above the ground. That might not sound like much but as a youngster the chickens were half my height! I saw them make grown people run screaming. It was quite a frightening sight.

My brother got The Roosters started on humans. He really thought it was funny the way they had all the four-legged animals living under the cars. The dogs and cats cowered under the cars. If they wanted to leave the yard, they bolted out from under the car as fast as their legs could carry them. The slower ones could only sneak from car to car as they tried to get to the edge of the yard where they had a sporting chance of getting away from The Roosters.

My brother taunted the chickens by sticking his foot out at them. That might not sound like much of a taunt, but The Roosters could not tolerate it. To the chickens, it must have been like someone flipping you the bird. If my brother just stuck his foot out, The Roosters would run all the way across the yard to attack him.

We often contemplated why such a thing occurred. Did the chickens think he was another rooster? Did they just think it was fun? It could have been possible they just thought my brother was crazy and they were going to get him before he got them.

My little sister was the first one The Roosters attacked unprovoked. They soon had her too scared to come out of the

house. I laughed until I became their target. I had to leave my bicycle close to the door so that I could run out and jump on it to make my escape. They still chased after me. I had to pedal with one foot while kicking at them with the other.

You might get the impression that The Roosters just hung around the house waiting for someone to come out. That would be correct. They were brutal. They were organized. My dad thought it was funny and for the most part, it was.

My mother said it was embarrassing when The Roosters started doing this stuff to total strangers. She said they had to go.

With those words, we stepped up our chicken eating program. Even at a chicken a week, it would still take us more than four months to finish off this gang of chickens. We had to double up. We had fried chicken (of course), chicken salad, chicken sandwiches, grilled chicken, boiled chicken, chicken pot pies, and chicken dishes that were new even to me.

That was when I really started detesting the smell of scalded chicken feathers.

A few more natural calamities dwindled The Rooster's numbers. One attacked my brother-in-law and he shot it. We ate a lot of them. Of course, that was natural for us, but a calamity for the chicken. A horse kicked one of them. As it turns out, horses do not have much tolerance for a chicken attack.

Over time, there was only this one rooster left. He was the meanest of the whole gang. Best watchdog we ever had, but still mean.

That's how we all came to look forward to a meal provided personally by this particular rooster. He was the last of a mean bunch.

On Saturday night, we went out to catch the rooster. You do this at night so that you can sneak up on the chickens. That's when they're all just sitting on their roost, resting. They don't like the dark so they go to roost as soon as the sun sets. Some chickens will go to roost during a solar eclipse.

"You boys ready to get that rooster?" My dad stood up from his chair and stretched. It was just shortly after dark. My brother and I nodded our heads. "Ya'll gotta be quiet. That white rooster is a sneaky one."

We sneaked down to the chicken pen, which was on this side of the outhouse and in front of the hog pen. We *ever* so quietly opened the gate and stepped into the pen. We were just three shadowy figures, creeping in the moonlight. We gingerly stuck our heads into the chicken coop, stopping to let our eyes adjust to the pitch-blackness inside.

The musty aroma of feathers and chicken-droppings permeated the air. Occasionally, we heard the questioning cluck of a suspicious hen. It was more of a "Brahhoock-brahock-broc". The exact spelling may vary with cultural differences.

Our eyes adjusted slowly to the dim light. We could barely see the fluffy, round shapes of the chickens perched on the roosts. My brother pointed to our left. A lighter colored chicken was roosting there. My dad slowly stretched out his hand. His hand eased towards the resting chicken. Then with a quick jerk, he had the rooster by the legs.

Or rather, by a leg – you would have thought that we were killing that chicken.

The rooster let out a screech that pierced the night air. Like a siren wail, it alerted every chicken in the chicken house. They flew straight towards the door as if they were all shot out from a cannon at the same time. They were getting out and they did not care that we were in the way!

I hope to this day that I am never, ever again pummeled by live, panic-stricken chickens.

It really was not painful – just frightening. The chickens' cackling was louder than race time at a dirt track. It sounded like a bunch of Chevys with cheap glass packs. Chickens were jumping all over the place. They were hitting us in the head, stomach, and feet. They were everywhere. My brother was yelling, my dad hollering, and I was screaming. The rooster was flapping his wings wildly. The dogs got scared and started barking from under the cars.

The four of us, my dad and brother, myself, and the rooster, fell backwards out of the chicken coop.

My dad was laughing so hard that he could barely hold onto the rooster.

We stuffed that bugger (the chicken, not my dad) into smaller accommodations for the night and on Sunday morning, the three of us returned for our dinner guest.

"Go get the rope and axe, Son." Unless you were going to hang it, that might seem like a strange combination to fetch for killing a chicken but they were both essential tools.

When I came back from collecting the tools, my dad took the rooster out of the pen. He held it by the legs, upside-down. The rooster did not say a word. He had his neck turned up, looking at us, staring suspiciously at us.

"Let me have one end of the rope." My dad tied the rope around one of the rooster's leg. "You hold onto that other end. We don't want him wandering off."

Chickens running around with their heads chopped off were highly unpredictable. They would always run somewhere inconvenient, like under the house. Once, one ran out into the road and a car ran over it. Not much you can do with that except kick it into the ditch.

"Can't we just tie the rope to something?" I asked, but it was too late. My dad already had the chicken laid across the chopping block. With a quick downward slash of the axe, the head was off.

My job was to hold onto the rope to keep the chicken from running off.

Blood squirted everywhere. The rooster jumped up and down, up and down. Holding onto the rope was a little spooky. Having a tug-of-war with an animal without a head was bad enough but sometimes the rooster ran straight at me as if it knew where I was. Finally, I could not take it any longer. I threw down the rope and ran screaming. My dad loved that. He slapped his knee and laughed so hard that tears came to his eyes.

That old geezer (again, the rooster not my dad) had the last laugh. The chicken was tougher than eating a retreaded tire.

I had this pet baby chick for a while. It was the only chicken with which I've ever felt an emotional tie. It was a little chick, just a few days old. I kept it in a birdcage in the house. I even trained it to follow me wherever I went. It just ran along right behind me.

Unfortunately, it could not tell the difference between me and everyone else.

It was following my sister around one day and she didn't know it. She stepped back and stepped directly on it – smashed it flatter than a flitter. We all know how flat that is. It left a greasy spot on the floor that didn't come up for months. It was a constant reminder.

I saw a drunken chicken once.

For some reason, we had a different chicken in a cage in the house. My dad had some homemade wine and poured the chicken a snout full. The chicken loved it. It would suck up a mouth full, stick its beak in the air, and guzzle it down. Soon it stopped, looked around, and started chirping like crazy.

"Chirp, chirp, chirp." It chirped loud, it chirped soft, it chirped in a whisper.

Then it started running. It ran about ten feet and fell over. It jumped up and fell over again. Then it started all over at the beginning. It soon got tired and just laid there on the kitchen floor where it fell.

It did not die though. Like most chickens, it just could not hold its liquor.

A high school buddy and I used to hunt and shoot for fun. We both had .22 caliber semi-automatic rifles with scopes. We mainly shot birds, squirrels, cans, pigeons, trees, and water – very few things that actually had a formal "season." Hunting seasons were for the city folk anyway.

On this particular day, we were walking in the woods, waiting for something to move, when we heard the rustling of leaves. We readied our rifles and cocked our hunters' heads to the side. Something was running straight towards us and it was coming fast!

Suddenly, out of the undergrowth, came a chicken!

Now this wasn't an ordinary chicken. It had a chicken body and it had a chicken head but the chicken head was not exactly attached to the chicken's body. It was flopping over to one side. It flopped and dangled with every stride that the chicken took. It looked like some kind of demon with feathers.

"What the hell is it?" My friend gripped my arm. He could barely whisper his query.

"I don't know, but it's not going to stop!" I did not like the looks of it. That monster was running right at us!

"Kill it!" he yelled. We opened fire until we emptied our guns. We were both shaking so much that I doubt we hit it. If we did, it did not slow down.

We did the only thing left to do. We ran as hard as we could and avoided that section of the woods for quite some time. My dad said that someone had probably wrung its neck, a common alternative to chopping off a chicken's head, and the chicken had gotten away.

"That wouldn't have happened if they'd tied a rope to its leg." Experience says it all.

Out where we lived, there were several commercial chicken houses. When it came time to collect the chickens, they too gathered them up at night.

"I dropped my chewing gum last night in the chicken house. I thought I found it three or four hundred times." My brother used to help them catch the chickens. He had to tell me that joke a few times before I finally caught onto the resemblance of chewing gum and chicken-droppings.

After one night of chicken catching, he brought home an extra. The chicken had escaped from the chicken house and they didn't catch it until after the big truck load of fryers had left. We put this extra chicken in a pen for a few days to fatten it up – after all these were fryers. Purebreds! Professionally trained chicken sandwiches!

This chicken took the "fatten-up" part all too seriously.

Between all of us (humans, that is), we had seen a passel of chickens but never had anyone seen a chicken that blowed up like this one. I know that "blowed up" isn't a proper term but it's the only phrase that truly described what happened. The drumsticks pumped up to about the size of a quart can of oil. The breasts poked out like the grill of a '57 Studebaker. It had a ravenous appetite, eating everything in sight. It actually swelled up so big that its legs could no longer support its weight and it just sat there and ate. Sometimes, it would kind of wiggle around from feeding spot to feeding spot.

We decided not to eat this monstrosity.

Soon, the chicken was double the weight and size of any chicken we'd ever seen. Then it died. Total time from birth to death by being fattened-up was less than six weeks.

We knew that the chicken had lived long beyond the time meant for human eyes. We didn't even speculate where that truck load of super-fattening fryers was going – or when and how we'd see them again.

It is always a good story to share over an order of chicken nuggets.

Southern Fried Recipe

Originally a Southern Fried <u>Chicken</u> recipe, Aunt Martha said that "chicken" narrowed the recipe down too much. She preferred "Southern Fried" and you fill in the gap. Be it chicken, vegetable, fish, turkey, an occasional possum, or you don't want to know what, the answer is simple – fry it.

For our recipe though, we'll use chicken.

Get 1 good sized chicken
Salt & Black Pepper
Flour
1 Cup of Grease (use almost a cup of Crisco and top off with bacon grease)

Clean the chicken and cut it up the way you like it. Roll the pieces around in the salt and a good quantity of black pepper to give it a little bite. Roll the chicken pieces in the flour and coat them well.

Heat the grease in an iron skillet. Put in a tiny piece of the skin and when it bubbles real good, the grease is ready.

Put the chicken pieces in the skillet but try not to let them touch while frying. Fry to golden color on that side and then turn it over. Lower the heat some and simmer on that side until golden brown. It should only take 35-40 minutes. If you see blood, turn over and cook some more.

Outhouse Blues

When I was a kid, Fall was my favorite time to go to the bathroom. In the summer, it was too hot and buggy. In the spring, everything was growing and the bumblebees were out. And winter – well – I just didn't like having to put on a coat to go to the bathroom, although it was interesting when it snowed.

Our outhouse was a bit of a walk from the main house. It was past the fig trees and the chicken coop, past the remnants of some ancestral stone barbecue pit, beyond the pecan trees and finally past the hog pen and there you were. It sounds farther than it really was. It was probably no more than fifty yards.

I really saved up to make it worth the trip.

I knew I had reached some degree of adulthood when I could no longer get anyone to go with me for a midnight call of nature.

My first trip alone was really quite frightening. When I reached the edge of the lawn, I stepped gingerly through the foot-tall jungle of growth. The sprinkling of dew was cool against my bare ankles. All was quiet around me except for the incessant chirping of the crickets. I kept up my creeping pace. My destiny lay ahead – the small, square building almost obscured from my sight even in the bright moonlight. My hand reached for the weathered wooden door with a small hole that served as a handle – an ingenious device by its sheer simplicity.

I slipped inside to total darkness.

My hand fumbled for the flashlight. Why hadn't I turned it on before I came in? Someone could be inside! My heart jumped into my throat. I was sure that I heard someone breathing.

Finally, the weak beam came on. The small room was empty, though no less frightening. Paper was strewn about the floor. Vines were growing in between planks on the side – no time to think about that. Get to business and get out.

All that just to go to the bathroom and then I couldn't go. It was too much excitement. I don't know why I was so scared. Even a psychopathic killer wouldn't hide in an outhouse. That really would have been crazy.

I did try a shortcut for a while. The shortcut was to just pee out my bedroom window. Of course, I was eventually caught. It turns out that urine eats right through screen wire and, as I found out, a good switch eats right through thin jeans!

You might have heard stories about people using the Sears and Roebuck catalog in outhouses. Personally, we didn't care for the catalogs too much. The glossy paper just wasn't very absorbent. Newspaper did a much more efficient job, especially if you crumpled it up and stretched it out a few times to soften the fibers.

I remember our first replacement outhouse. I was five at the time. It technically wasn't new. Some people my dad knew were getting inside plumbing and didn't need their outhouse anymore. I begged for an inside bathroom and my dad finally told me that we couldn't have an inside bathroom because you had to have running water first.

One thing just leads to another.

Before you have running water, you also need drains. At the time, our kitchen didn't even have a sink. The countertop was just flat. We kept a bucket in the kitchen that we filled with water we drew from the well. It was my chore to keep the bucket full with that cool, pure water.

Well, almost pure water.

That's one of the problems with water direct from the ground; you never know what the water travels through before it gets to your well. In our case, the water must have traveled through some sort of sulfur pocket, because it always had a slight sulfur smell to it. Whenever you took a drink, you had to hold your breath to keep from smelling it. Luckily, it didn't have the sulfur taste. All the same, we mostly drank tea.

Drawing water was a fairly simple task. When I got big enough, it became a chore on my list. Our back porch was built around the well. All I had to do was open the cover to the well, drop the bucket down, and then haul it back up full of water. To draw up the water bucket, there was the typical small log with a handle that served as a windlass. As you turned the handle, the rope would wind around the log assisted by a pulley attached to the ceiling of the porch. One time my hand slipped off and the handle spun around faster than I could get out of the way. It came around and smacked me right in the mouth – splitting my lip and chipping two of my front teeth.

My dad said it was a learning experience. I learned well enough that it never happened to me again!

Inside our house was a community water dipper used for drinking. Outside we had two dippers – one for the family and one for the workers who helped us. As strange as it might sound, there were people who were much worse off than we were and whom we could actually afford to pay to help us out on the farm.

Nowadays I doubt if you could even find a water dipper.

A portion of what we paid the help came in the form of food. Being on the farm, we certainly had food. My dad's idea of a small garden was about ten acres of corn and five acres of other vegetables. My mother spent most of the summer canning. She canned tomatoes, green beans, bread-and-butter pickles, okra (pickled okra was the best), and whatever else we grew.

My favorite time of all was when she canned jellies and jams. In the fall, we would ride the horses over the mountain and pick muscadines. This sweet wild grape had a tough and slightly bitter skin but inside was a rich, juicy pulp. It makes my mouth water just thinking about it. My mom used about half of our haul to make muscadine jelly and my dad used the other half for homemade wine.

When my mother cooked the muscadines for jelly, it would form a foam that would turn semi-solid when it cooled. You could not preserve the foam through canning so we had to eat it all. She would cook up some hot biscuits and we would sop up the muscadine jelly foam. Whoa! You talk about some good eating! We would have a whole meal of hot biscuits and jelly foam.

Good ol' jelly foam. You can't buy it or steal it. You just have to live it.

Finally, that new, second-hand outhouse broke down. I mean *literally* broke down. It collapsed. It just started leaning sideways and eventually fell over. If you have never seen the underside of an outhouse, don't feel bad. There are a lot of old folks who've never seen the underside either. Amazingly, it's quite clean and dry. It shows that someone picked a good spot for it many years ago.

I am sure those spiders and bugs helped keep it clean, too.

Some kids pulled a big prank when I was in high school. They broke into the school and filled it up with goats, chickens, sheep, and every other animal they could find, catch, or steal. The pièce de résistance was an old outhouse dumped right in the middle of the school lobby in front of the cafeteria. The students, and most of the teachers, thought it was pretty funny. I thought it was funny too, until I realized that this outhouse was in better shape than our outhouse. I thought about volunteering to help clean, hoping I'd get to haul the outhouse away. I was afraid that I would just look like I was brown-nosing. Even today, I can still imagine my mom and dad's face if I had pulled into the driveway with a new bathroom – a free new bathroom!

They would have been proud of their boy.

My dad saved us though. He found another outhouse – a real gem! A two-seater! I thought a two-seater was a little strange. Who would want to sit in an outhouse and do his or her business with somebody else? Strange begets stranger because later I saw a three-seater.

There is nothing like a new bathroom to add value to your home.

This two-seater outhouse was probably less than ten years old to boot. Why would anyone get rid of a quality building like that? We couldn't figure. Even if you were getting indoor plumbing, it was still a good building. You could put your lawn mower or hand tools in it and sit down while you worked. It would make a real nice building for shovels, rakes, and other tall tools. We lucked out!

I went along with my dad and brother-in-law to bring the building home.

"What kind of tools do we need to fetch an outhouse?" My brother-in-law stumbled a little on the word "tools." The word had not crossed his lips enough times for him to be used to the pronunciation.

My dad was backing the truck up to the barn where we kept our tools. "In general, you use tools that you don't care too much about. You don't want to mess up your good stuff."

"That's easy for me then – I don't care too much about any tool." My brother-in-law was, at least, honest.

We returned a few hours later with the outhouse on the back of our pickup.

"While you have it on the truck, why don't you move it closer to the house?" My mother said, as she came out to see our find before we unloaded it.

"Well, if we do that, we'll have to dig a new pit. We can always dig the pit later and then move the outhouse." None of us really wanted to dig a new outhouse pit and my mother knew it would never be moved. Once an outhouse was put down, we'd never known anyone to move one. In fact, I'm sure that it's bad luck.

At least that's what my dad told my mother when she brought up the subject again.

We chopped down all the trees and bushes that had grown up around the old outhouse as the new one had a bigger footprint. We unloaded it, leveled it, and got out the lawnmower to cut the grass leading to it. We were proud of that new building.

I couldn't wait to use it, but I wanted it all to myself. I wasn't comfortable using it with everyone standing around watching. They'd ask you how it was when you came out and was it better than the old one. The rest of the family didn't seem to mind, but I really wanted to experience it privately.

When it was close to dark, I finally got my chance. I dropped my drawers and hopped up on the seat on the right hand side. I had to slide back a little to get comfortable when it happened. Where the boards came together on the seat, there was a crack. The boards shifted and pinched me right between the legs. It was one of those blood-blistering pinches in a place that you can't see unless you're some kind of contortionist.

Believe you me – I made a mental note about the hole on that side.

After one of my sisters got a job, she was going to have some friends come over to spend the weekend. That was the second time I remember cutting the grass to the outhouse. My dad even bought a real toilet seat and nailed it to one side so that the girls would not blood-blister pinch themselves.

I thought that was nice.

In dry spells and with the right placement you could even build a tower over the course of several days. It gave a boy something to do during summer vacation. I had visions of building a tower all the way to the butt portal but the turd stools always tipped over before they got very tall.

We had a neighbor who kept his dogs on the lean side. He always said that it made them into better hunters if they were a little hungry. One day I was in the outhouse and I heard something under me. One of my big fears was that a snake would be under there and bite me on my bottom. I jumped off the seat so fast that I almost hurt myself. I looked in through the hole and saw one of the neighbor's dogs under there. I wish I could say he was getting in out of the rain but instead he was having a picnic. I inadvertently left his master a little surprise on top of his head.

Always think twice before you let your dog lick your face.

We did eventually put in a bathroom. I came home from college one weekend to help put it in. We enclosed a portion of the back porch and put the bathroom there. The bathroom door opened to the porch so technically we still had to go outside to get to the inside bathroom. It was several years later before we added the tub. To this day, I have not taken more than a sponge bath at my parents' house and I lived there for eighteen years.

My dad was worried that the well could not support the water requirements for the new bathroom. Over time, sand and dirt had crept into the well and made it more shallow. The fix was to clean out the well and make it deeper. You can look in the yellow pages all day long and you won't find a single well maintenance man. Sure, you'll find those places that will drill a new well. They put in that wimpy kind with an eight or ten-inch diameter hole but there isn't anyone to clean out a real well like ours.

Our well was about five feet across and about forty feet down before you came to the water. They had to be big because all the wells were hand dug in those days. The well size had to be big enough for a man and shovel to fit into it with enough room left over to dig. The sides of the well had hand and foot steps dug into it to make it easier for the well diggers to climb in and out. Towards the bottom, the well flared out to be even bigger in diameter. It was almost like a shelf that went all the way around. It was dug far enough into the earth that a man could actually hide by sitting on the dirt shelf and pulling up his legs. It was also very cool deep in the well. We knew that the shelf had once been used to store perishable items like milk and such to keep them from spoiling. There were even stories that the shelf had once been used to hide a couple of Confederate soldiers from Union troops but we had no proof of that.

My description of the inside of the well isn't second hand information. When you can't find anyone to clean out a well and you have a teenage son, then your problem is easily solved. My dad certainly wasn't going down into the well and my friend Roy, who helped us on the weekends, was scared to death of going down, so I was the only remaining choice.

Starting early on a Saturday morning, they lowered me into the well along with a short handled shovel. The water in the well was indeed shallow. By standing on the dirt shelf, I would fill up a five-gallon bucket with mud from the bottom of the well. My dad and Roy would haul out the bucket and send another one down. It was a slow go. Getting in and out was very hard, so at lunchtime, they just sent down a sandwich and I ate it in the bottom of the well. Occasionally, I would get a feeling of claustrophobia. I was working in a small muddy area with only a flashlight to provide light. Above me, the opening to the well seemed small and so far away. Sometimes I could see a head peering down at me, but anything they said echoed so badly it was difficult to understand.

I didn't know it at the time, but my mother was near hysterics from worrying about me. She was afraid that the sides of the well would cave in or that I would hit a major vein of water and the well would fill up before they could get me out. Being young and adventurous, none of that ever crossed my mind.

"Heads up! I got something special coming down for you." It was mid-afternoon when Roy called down. He lowered the bucket and sure enough inside the bucket was four little bottles of Miller High Life beer.

That certainly hit the spot.

I had dug out about three feet of dirt at the time. I took a break and drank my Millers. I went back to work and dug out two shovels of dirt when I finally hit one of the underground streams that fed the well. The stream of water was about two inches in diameter. I kept digging and hit two smaller streams of water. Now the race was on! I had to dig out as much dirt as possible before the well filled up.

Above me, I heard a sudden heard a rush of excitement. I looked up in time to see both my dad and Roy's heads disappear from sight. I could hear them both talking to my mother. I couldn't hear what they said, but I could tell that they were talking urgently.

"Hey! What's going on up there?" I yelled, but there was no reply. Meantime, the water was rising in the well, my bucket was full, but there was no one to retrieve the bucket – or me!

I then heard a car and it sounded like it was going fast. There was the sound of tires sliding on gravel and a couple of other excited voices. I could distinctly hear a woman crying.

To put my situation into perspective: I had been down in the bottom of a well since early that morning. I had just finished four beers. The well was filling up with water. It was impossible for me to get out by myself. My only contacts with the outside world had just disappeared and evidently, there was a lot of excitement going on above.

I was alone.

All I could do was to keep yelling "Hey!" But no one came.

It felt like an eternity but turned out to only be about ten minutes. Roy finally popped his head into the opening. "You okay?"

"Yeah, what's going on?"

It turned out that a neighbor's little girl had been thrown off a horse and we were the closest house with a telephone. They had the girl in the car and were on the way to the hospital. They stopped at our house so we could call ahead to the hospital and they could call in one of the doctors. They took off again in the car while my dad telephoned the hospital. He also called the State Patrol and arranged for them to meet and escort the family.

The little girl had a concussion but was otherwise okay.

About six o'clock that evening, they finally pulled me out of the well. As far as I know, that was the last time the well was cleaned.

I crossed off another profession from my list of possibilities.

I once asked my mother why my dad had not put in a bathroom earlier in our lives. After all, we had plenty of horses that he could have sold to have one installed.

"That was my fault," my mother said.

"Why was it your fault? You asked him many times to put in one."

"That's the reason. I pestered him so much about it that it became a point of principle for him. Until I quit nagging, he wasn't going to put in a bathroom."

You have to admire a man who sticks to his principles.

It never seemed to bother my dad that we had an outhouse. He started the Humane Society in the county and was very active in the American Cancer Society. He had influential friends in political positions, and was asked to run as a deputy sheriff one election year because of the votes he could draw. These people and others were often at the house. When they had to go to the bathroom, it never bothered my dad to point them towards the back door and tell them to follow the path. In fact, my dad seemed to take some pleasure in bringing these people back down to earth – so to speak.

Hot Day Recipe

There aren't many foods that go with outhouse stories. According to Aunt Martha, something fried would work. However, I do have one, very memorable taste experience to share.

Get an 8 pack of little Millers (not Miller Lite)
Ice
Well Bucket

Put the little Millers in the bottom of the well bucket. Cover with ice. Lower well bucket to well digger in well. Wait to pull up empties.

The well digger will appreciate it.

Red Eyes at Night

One early spring when I was about ten years old, the weather had warmed up, the grass was growing, and the time had just sprang forward. My dad and I were working one Saturday trying to get a head start on clearing a section of pastureland.

As usual, we were running late. My mom was the schedule keeper. She kept up with where we needed to be at a particular time. My dad always promised to be home at that time, but we just seldom made it.

"When you work with horses, cows, and the outdoor elements, it's hard to make everything cooperate." My dad tried to explain to my mother, but it was a constant battle between time and schedule.

Tonight, we were running late for a Saturday night oyster stew. I personally did not mind. Oyster stew was not to my taste. I preferred a big glass of milk with hot cornbread crumbled into it. That was eating!

My dad was driving our old tractor and pulling a two-wheeled wagon behind it that contained our tools and me. It was almost pitch dark and we still had a ways to go before getting to the house.

My dad looked around at me. I could tell that he was asking me a question but the tractor was so loud that he finally had to shut off the engine.

"Did you yell, Son?"

"No, Sir. I didn't say anything."

"I coulda' sworn I heard someone yelling."

My father stood up on the footboards of the tractor, straining to see into the darkness. The battery was always weak so the tractor's headlights were beginning to dim with the engine off. He switched off the lights and we were in almost complete darkness.

I thought it was a little creepy before but this was ridiculous!

Then, we heard a man yell, "Hey! Where are you?"

"Here!" We could just make out an image coming towards us. At first, all we noticed was the swinging beam of the flashlight. Our beagle was with us and he didn't bark, so we figured it must be somebody he knew.

"I been looking for y'all a long time. I heard you hollering but I couldn't find you. The sound kept playing tricks on me." It was my brother-in-law, Andy. Andy was here for the oyster stew. My mother sent him down in the pasture to look for us.

"We didn't yell. We were way past the second creek. That last holler you let loose was the only one that I heard." My dad grunted a little as he climbed down from the tractor.

"Naw! I've been hollering at you for almost fifteen minutes. It'd sound like I was getting close and then you'd sound like you were a long ways off. I was beginning to think you were playing games with me." Andy liked using his hands when he talked. Even now, as he was lighting a cigarette, he incorporated the hand motions into the conversations – alternating between waving a lit match and an unlit cigarette.

"You say you called us?" This was starting to interest my father. He walked a little closer to Andy. I quickly climbed out of the wagon and followed close behind. I might have been ten years old but I still didn't care much for being in the dark alone.

"Yes." Andy blew out a stream of smoke. He had finally gotten the cigarette lit.

"And you say we answered back?" My dad had a quizzical look on his face.

"'Yeah." Andy took a drag on the cigarette and his face was momentarily lit up in an orange glow.

"And you were doing that for fifteen minutes or so?" Something just wasn't adding up for my dad.

"It couldn't have been us. We were on the tractor. Might be 'coon hunters but I doubt it. You been drinking, Andy?" My father wasn't implying that Andy was a drunk – Andy just enjoyed life and some days he enjoyed it more than everyone else.

"Naw, Ray. I haven't had more than a couple of beers. Here let me holler again and I'll show you." Andy had a voice for hollering and he let loose a good one.

And we answered!

Well, it wasn't us but *someone* hollered back. Instead of a holler though, it sounded more like a scream. It made the hair on the back of my neck stand up like the barber's clippers did when I'd get a haircut. I was just glad that it sounded so far away.

"Dang! Who do you think it is? The way they're screaming, you'd think they were hurt. They must be way over the hill. Yell again, Andy." My father knew who had the best yelling voice.

Andy let loose another good holler. He was answered, only this time the scream was much closer!

"That didn't quite sound like a person, Andy." My dad echoed my thoughts exactly. "Sounded more like a baby crying real loud." He didn't have to say that. A crying baby scared me anytime.

"What do you mean it's not a person? What else could it be? Here, I'll do it again." Andy enjoyed any opportunity for a good holler.

After Andy's third holler, the scream was even closer!

"One more time, Andy! Whatever it is, it's coming down that hill fast!"

Andy hollered one last time. The returning scream sounded like it was right in front of us! The sound shrilled my ears like no baby I'd ever met! I moved in closer to the bigger folks. They were staring intensely into the brush on the side of the trail.

All of a sudden, Andy pointed and whispered, "There it is!"

Sure enough, in the dim light, we could see two red eyes staring back at us from within the brush.

I couldn't see much but I could tell that the eyes were taller than me!

My father reached over and flicked on the headlights of the tractor. The trees and bushes in front of us were immediately lit up. The eyes flashed bright and fuzzy for a split second and then, with a rustle of leaves, they were gone.

My dad switched off the lights and we saw nothing.

"Call him again, Andy!" I couldn't believe my dad said that. It was gone and we should all be glad.

Andy hollered again and this time the returning scream was back up high on the hill. It was getting farther away and I was so glad.

Being comfortable with its distance, I eased back to the wagon and fumbled around until I found the axe and a hammer.

I returned to my place between my dad and Andy. My dad looked down and I handed him the axe. He hesitated a moment but then seemed to see the merit in it. He took the axe. I kept the hammer. I heard a click and saw Andy had opened his pocketknife. We weren't going down easily!

When Andy hollered again, the answering scream was close. We could hear an occasional light crack of a twig.

We couldn't see it at first but then there appeared two tiny sparkles of red glistening in the night air. They got brighter and closer and the red eyes were once again staring at us through the dark of night.

I gripped my hammer tightly and didn't breathe – couldn't breathe. My dad had both hands on the axe but he finally tore one away and flicked on the tractor lights.

The eyes flashed and were gone.

We called it down from that hill a number of times. Each time, it came in until we could see its bright red eyes but we never did see it. Finally, we couldn't call it down any more.

That was fine with me. I thought this whole thing had gone too far and too long.

The story was the hit of the oyster stew supper that night. It somewhat redeemed us for being so late. It taught me a good lesson – if you're going to be late, you'd better have a good story. This one was a doozy!

We told our story anytime more than two people got together – weddings, funerals, or reunions. There were all sorts of speculation. Some thought it was a rabid raccoon (any raccoon that does anything to be noticed is rabid). A coyote was suggested but we knew they only lived way out west. Some folks hinted at things more supernatural and that scared me all over again.

Andy announced that he was sure it was an alien from outer space. At the time, he had just purchased some school buses that he was converting into barns for emus.

The most prevalent explanation was a panther. One person claimed to have seen a black panther crossing the road. Some tracks had been found, we just weren't sure if the tracks were a panther or a beaver.

The next Friday night, my mom, dad, and I were watching TV. My sisters were all out with their friends. My dad had parched some peanuts in the oven and we were eating those with some cold Coca-Colas.

It was getting late, and my eyes were sleepy, but I was determined to stay awake to see Ed Sullivan.

"You think he's asleep?" My dad asked my mom. I assumed he was referring to me.

I immediately went into my "pretend to sleep" mode. I was quite adept at pretending to be asleep. I learned a lot from it. It doesn't work now. If I pretend to be asleep now, I really go to sleep.

"I think so. Robert? Robert?" My mom asked it so that if I were awake I would hear her but not so loud as to wake me up if I were asleep. It was a delicate balance.

"Robert?" She asked one more time.

"Huh?" I muttered a muffled reply as if I was mostly asleep. This was my art.

"He's asleep." She confirmed my art.

"Turns out that Andy may have been right." My dad said ominously.

"You mean there really are catfish the sizes of submarines in Lake Buckhorn that will eat the flesh off of you?"

From her voice inflection, I could almost hear her eyebrows rising up when she said that.

"No. No. Not that." My dad kind of chuckled. "I mean about the red eyes we saw down in the pasture. I was telling a salesman about it today at the drugstore. He was from Ohio and he said that a similar creature was seen there. They called it Moth Man. Seems that this Moth Man has red eyes just like ours and is fast. He also has wings." My dad let that trail off for effect.

"They think Moth Man is an alien. He attacked some folks in a car and scared a lot of others. The wings would sure explain how that thing got up the hill so fast. No panther could have travelled that far that fast.

"I didn't want to mention it in front of Robert. He's already too scared to go to the bathroom at night." I heard him crack a couple of peanut shells as he finished up his story.

And how right he was!

I was afraid to go outside, in the dark, away from the lights of the house, in the middle of the night, to go to the bathroom. It had nothing to do with red eyes or Moth Man or anything recent. I feared Vampires, Wolfman, Frankenstein, and various creatures of the night for a long time before Moth Man came along.

Of course, *now*, I was even more scared and I couldn't say anything. Moth Man might be scary but letting my parents know I was playing possum was even scarier. I stayed quiet.

When I went to bed that night, I immediately went into my most protective sleep position. I curled into a ball and crossed my forearms in front of my neck. Let a vampire or Moth Man try to suck blood through that!

Now, fifty years later, when I'm out in the woods at night alone, even if I know that the security of our modern life is only a few yards away, I think about that night. The hairs on my neck stand up and I wonder what is watching us from the woods, waiting for us to make a mistake.

I've had that feeling when driving alone late at night on a lonely road on a cool evening with things around you in the woods. It's not fear as much as a feeling of smallness and not knowing what all is really there.

Sometimes my thoughts take me back to that night. I see everything so vividly – my father, Andy, the piercing red eyes and even the old 8N Ford tractor. Sometimes, just for a fleeting second, I feel like I'm there. Seeing it from the eyes of a ten year old boy and living it for the first time.

Out there somewhere, there is an explanation for those red eyes. It might be a panther but I doubt it. It might have been Moth Man, or a close relative of his, maybe a second cousin.

I still occasionally wake up at night with my arms crossed over my neck in my protective mode. It's not that I'm afraid of vampires, werewolves, or Moth Man – but why take chances?

Milk and Bread

Not being a connoisseur of Oyster Stew, I can't attest to any oyster stew recipes. However, I can attest to Milk and Bread! Give it a try. My dad and I could finish off a whole gallon of milk and a pone of cornbread in one sitting.

Get some cornbread
Milk
Tasty small sides (green peppers, green onions, or even radishes)

Make the cornbread. There are a lot of cornbread recipes but I've found that the one on the side of the cornmeal bag works as well as any.

While the cornbread is hot, crumble it into a big tea glass. Pour the milk over the cornbread (my mom preferred buttermilk).

Eat it with a long ice tea spoon and the small sides Fry up some streak-o-lean bacon as a small side for a real treat!

Horse Tales

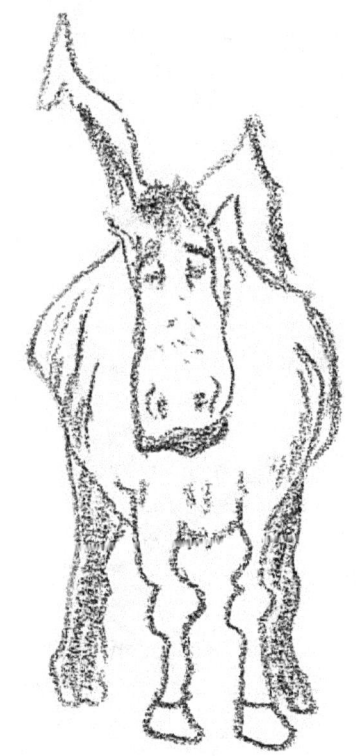

The cool evening air blew softly across my cheek, betraying the tiny drop of sweat running down my neck. There was a crisp chill in the air that brought a briskness to everyone's mood. All about was an undercurrent of excitement. Idle banter was a little too funny.

I was checking my tack for the third time. I did not like the looks of the tie strap, but it would hold for tonight. My dad and Roy were doing the same thing. We were trying something we had never tried before – each of us would be riding a green, unbroken horse that night.

There are a variety of horses. Some are babies that just want you to dote over them and rub 'em and just stand around them. Others bolt at the mere sight of a human. Lazy, high-strung, strong, or hard working – they are all different. Some are crazy because of the way they were raised and some are crazy because of their blood. A few want to kill you. Fewer are wonderful. Occasionally one will be loyal and protective. A couple you will love. Mostly, they're just like people.

Now you might think that an unbroken horse would be wild and cagey and would run over a transfer truck to get to you and trample you to death. However, most aren't. They're usually just big dogs who have grown up without any attention. That's the way these three were tonight. They were easy to catch. We'd put a saddle on them several times. You could lead them. These were all good signs, but we had not been on their backs before.

At this point, an analytical man would ask, "Why?" Not a troublesome question at all. My dad was somewhat of a jack-of-all-trades. He supplemented his livelihood with these odd jobs. Breaking horses was one of the jobs. We broke a lot of horses. After we had a horse for a month, you could put your kid on it – given the right temperament, opportunity, and kid. We rode until eleven or twelve o'clock at night many days of the week. I remember my mom getting upset with my dad for keeping me out so late.

Most folks never think about the work that goes into a horse to make it roadworthy. We'd each wiped a lot of blood off ourselves while on horseback, or under a horse, or beside a horse. Noses, fingers, toes – I even had my cheek ripped open by a horse. Therefore, the answer to "Why?" is simple. It was fun.

Regardless of the fun, we had taken on more than we could handle. My dad did not like to say "No" to anyone. We were behind schedule, so we were trying this new idea of three pre-green-broke horses at one time.

They were all mares. I had a buckskin, a beautifully built quarter horse. Roy had a pinto. She was a stubby type horse, short and very wide. My dad had a sorrel mare. She was a little horse who showed signs of being a good racking horse.

"I'm glad I just plowed that field in front of the house. It'll be a good place to start. Dirt's too deep for 'em to buck hard and it's nice and soft to land on." My dad looked at both of us. "We gotta get that crop in the ground next week."

"What kind of work are we raising this year, Mr. Ray? You can call it corn, peas, hay, butterbeans, cotton, or a crop – all we ever really raise is work." I always thought Roy had a realistic way of looking at things. He was impartial to any crop.

My dad chuckled. "Son, you go first. Roy, you get on the right side. Take this long rope and hook it onto her bridle. Son, when you go to get on, get on quick! Hit the saddle and grab hold of something, fast!"

We positioned ourselves around the horse. I really thought that we were over reacting. I had put the saddle on her dozens of times. I had shaken a sack at her until she stood stone dead still. I babied her. I gave her the best sweet feed. I covered her with a blanket to keep her coat shiny. I worked her on a lunge line every day to keep her muscles in good shape. She was in great shape. Look at those muscle lines.

Look at those muscles! She could stomp me!

Now I was nervous. Weakness in a horse could be an excellent quality right now.

I followed my dad's advice. I leaped into the saddle. In those days, I could do things like that – leap. The horse did not move. My feet found the stirrups. She still did not move. My hand found the saddle horn. I suddenly felt a mild electrical shock go through my body. The horse moaned like a – well – like a bucking horse.

I had the fleeting thought that maybe it was I who was actually saddled. That was one of the exciting parts of riding a horse for the first time. You really did not want to do it. The horse wanted you off. You wanted off, too, but getting off was scarier than staying on. I usually tried to stay on at all costs.

The horse leaped and landed stiff-legged three times in a row. She tried to rear up on her back legs but the soft dirt thwarted her efforts. All she accomplished was hitting me in the

nose with her head. At times like this, you don't even notice a
bloody nose.

The soft dirt worked. She ended up falling down. I just
spread my legs and stood over her. When she stood up, I was still
in the saddle. She kept bucking until she fell a couple of more
times and then she stood still. I sat on her very still. Roy was still.
My dad was still. My mother was on the porch and she was still.
It was one of those still moments that are etched in your mind
forever like a photograph. I don't know why. It's probably taking
up room in my brain that could be used for something useful.

My dad whispered to Roy, "Now, get your horse."

Roy eased into his saddle uneventfully and breathed a
sigh of relief – his last for the evening.

My dad slowly crept over to his horse. He grabbed hold
of the horse's bridle cheek strap, pulled the horse's head over
until it touched the saddle, and then he mounted. In case you
haven't ridden much, you can't ride a horse far in that position.
You eventually have to let go or you just kind of go around in a
small circle. So, my dad had to let go. We watched his hand
intently – like it was a fuse on a bomb.

"You ready?" I looked at my dad and saw a sparkle in his
eyes. I knew that he loved this moment. It was exciting. It was
scary. It was living.

All bombs have their moment.

My dad's horse took one giant leap forward. It might
have covered twenty feet. I saw very little of what happened to

my dad after that for I had my own problems. My horse jumped forward and ran right over Roy and his horse.

The horses that Roy and I were riding headed due north in front of the house. My dad's horse headed south behind the house. This might sound sort of casual but we didn't have much to do with the directions. I had my horse's head pulled all the way to her chest. Roy's horse had taken the bit in her mouth and was crow hopping as fast as mine could run. When we topped the hill, Roy and his ride set off in an easterly direction. I could tell by the dust more than anything else.

My dad's horse had already gone past the outhouse, past the plum bushes, and was making a full circle back to the front of the house.

We spent more than an hour and a half just trying to regroup. Sometimes two of us would get together and then the third would come and instead of stopping, his horse would just run right on by. It would not even look over at us. That'd get the other two started all over again.

My mother enjoyed it. She just sat down on the porch swing and watched the whole thing. From a spectator's point of view, we were probably entertaining.

Finally, we were all three together with the horses stopped.

"One minute you were all here and then the two of you were over the hill and the other headed down towards the creek." My mother was still laughing. We were exhausted.

"Well, I believe that's enough for tonight, boys." Roy and I dismounted quickly before my dad could change his mind.

As we were unsaddling, my dad said he was glad I stayed on the horse when it fell. "This is very important in training a horse. If a horse throws you off, bluffs you, scares you, or intimidates you in any way – it will remember. It will try it again, and again, and again for the rest of its life. A horse has a great mind for remembering what worked once, but it never learns when it stops working. I've owned horses for twenty years that pulled the same tricks for twenty years. Pull my finger." My dad stuck his index finger out to Roy.

Roy laughed. "Good example, Mr. Ray."

"What example, Roy? Really, pull my finger."

The next night, I couldn't even get close to my horse. She saddled well. No problem there. But when I went to get on, she dragged all three of us out across the field. When we finally got her stopped, my dad got out the "twister." Some people call it the "twitch." They are equally humane. I prefer "twister." A twister is a two-foot piece of wood with a loop of rope attached to one end. An old posthole digger handle makes the best handle. The loop is about as big around as your fist. You stick your hand through the loop, grab hold of the horse's nose, pull it through the loop, and then twist around and around on the handle. Hence – "twister".

A twister is like Valium to a horse.

"This'll take her mind off what we're doing," my dad said as he twisted her nose into the shape of a tennis ball. There's a small part in all of us that enjoys doing that sort of thing a little too much. My sisters liked to tickle the horse's nose with their fingernails when it was like that, so I know this is not just a masculine/feminine trait.

A week later, they were all riding respectably.

"I believe that I've got this one under control now, Mr. Ray." Roy was hot-dogging it a little in the middle of the road. "Look at this, power steering!"

That little horse must have been waiting for that moment all week. As soon as Roy relaxed one muscle, she knew it. She immediately started spinning around and around in the middle of the road. It caught Hotdog Roy off guard and he tumbled to the ground.

In two more weeks, those horses were well behaved, dependable mounts and we were off to different horses. I've forgotten more of those horses than I can remember.

Those were some long nights on horseback. Three people riding together night after night could get monotonous. The horses had a way of generating excitement from time to time but we were mostly just putting miles and manners on horses so others could ride them. It's a job that's not appreciated very often. We rode down old roads and old sawmill trails. We were rained on and thrown off. We were often very, very sore.

We purposefully rode through places that would frighten a horse. The more experiences they had, the calmer they would be when the new, maybe less experienced rider had control. Most of the horses we rode could be, and were, turned over to children when we were through.

The worst of all horses though, were the horses that were just plain slow. They didn't want to keep up and didn't have a lot of energy. When you rode one, the horse wore you out from the incessant urging, prodding, and kicking just to keep up with the other horses. However, there was a market for those horses.

Sometimes a horse that just follows is a good trait, especially for young riders.

Over the years, there were a lot of horses – Sandy, Tulip, Scout, Babe, Red, Stupid (for internal use only), Dillon, Blaze, and so many more horses long forgotten. Good horses. Horses that brought happiness to couples, children, family, and friends.

That's what my dad believed in. He worked hard to match people with the right animals and to match animals with the right people.

We had a colt once with an injured right front ankle. The colt had been in a remote pasture and the injury must have existed for some time before we discovered it. Any practical farmer would have put the poor thing out of its misery.

Not my dad. We spent hours getting the colt home, hours treating the injured ankle, hours feeding and caring for the animal. We called him Sonny.

Despite the vet's prognosis, the ankle healed. It was larger than the other ankle and, of course, the horse could never be ridden hard by any means but he was out of pain and well fed.

The constant nurturing he received because of his ankle also made him tolerant to almost anything. You could touch any leg and he would hold up his foot for you. He would doze off if you rubbed him between his ears. If you were in the pasture, he would leave the other horses to be with you. He would follow you around and minded better than the dogs we had – especially since he didn't bark.

My dad found Sonny a home. He sold him to a family with several kids. They didn't have much money so he sold it to them on credit. He had them purchase the tack as the down payment – fifty dollars. They were to pay five dollars a month over three years. So, over three years, that's $230 dollars. Not much money for all that trouble.

The horse was great with their kids. They could climb all over him. They let him live in the yard most of the time and he sometimes stuck his head neck right in the front door but never quite went inside.

My dad sent me to collect the payments three times in the first six months. He repossessed the horse at the end of eight months because they were behind on payments and were just not taking care of him.

We brought Sonny home to take better care of him and theirs kids were upset! The parents promised my dad they would take better care of him. They caught up the payments, but my dad didn't let Sonny go home with them until Sonny had fattened up some.

My dad threw in regular and free hoof trimmings. I knew it was so he could keep an eye on the horse – I also knew I would be the one who would have to do the trimming.

Any way you look at it, my dad lost money on that deal but it wasn't always about money with him. The animals came first, usually.

My dad always had dogs, too. When I was very young, he had a dog named "Jip".

I always called Jip my dog but he was clearly my dad's dog. Wherever my dad went, Jip was right there with him. Jip could be sound asleep but he would still hear my dad's footsteps and run to the back door waiting on him.

If my dad took a step towards the barn, Jip was there, sniffing around, looking for anything. If he took a step towards the pasture, Jip was there, checking out the bushes.

I have no idea what breed he was and I haven't seen a dog quite like him since. He had thick, but not long, red fur. He was a heavily built dog. I'm sure he looked big to me since I was only five or six years old. Adjusting for age though, Jip was about 50-60 pounds. His jaws were strong and his snout was similar to a retriever. I remember he had a big head! I even had a big, red marble that I named Jip – still have it.

Jip hated snakes.

When we would go near the creeks, Jip was on the hunt. He would sniff them out, hunt them down, and dig them out. Whatever he had to do to get to a snake, he did it. He barked and growled the whole time.

When he finally caught the snake, he was very adept at killing it. Jip would bite the snake behind its head and then shake his head back and forth, slinging the snake around until the snake was dead. He really hated snakes.

Jip tolerated me. He let me pet him and I could crawl all over him. Let my dad stand up though and I was sent tumbling, because Jip was going with my dad.

One Sunday morning we had just finished breakfast when my dad heard Jip barking. Jip had a lot of barks and we all recognized his alarm bark.

"Wild dogs!" My dad was looking out the kitchen window and out across the pasture.

I climbed up on the kitchen counter so I could see. There in the pasture was our horse Sunshine and her colt. A pack of wild dogs was attacking the colt.

This was before there were leash laws and animal control. When people got tired of their pets, they took them out to the country to unload. They didn't give a second thought to the consequences. These dogs now became the problem of every farmer and rural resident in the area.

Dogs just suddenly appeared. We would hear a strange car coming down the road late at night and, the next day, the community had a new canine resident, only no one wanted him.

A dumped dog has only a few options. The lucky ones get accepted by some family and live happily ever after. That happens a lot more in movies than it does in real life.

The tragic ones, but maybe the second most lucky, meet a quick death. This could be from cars, hunters, or neighbors with a strict no trespassing rule.

The least fortunate ones die a slow death from starvation, disease, or poisoning.

The group that's left become the real menace, for they are the survivors. They are strong enough and smart enough to survive on their own. They become the wild dogs – the mad dogs. They breed and multiply. They revert to their pack instincts. They have to eat, so they begin to kill. Chickens, goats, calves, and foals were all tasty meals to them. Once they taste blood, there's no going back for them. They even kill when they aren't hungry.

These were the dogs in the pasture attacking the mare and her colt.

My dad moved fast. He grabbed the shotgun and a box of shells. As he ran across the yard towards the pasture, the box of shotgun shells slipped from his hands and scattered across the ground.

"Grab the rest of the shells!" My dad yelled back at me. He had two shells in his hand and was already loading the gun.

Jip ran past me like a bullet. He was running so fast that his fur looked like waves flowing across his body. He ran past my dad and slammed chest first into one of the wild dogs. Jip and the dog were in a furious snarl.

I scrambled along the ground, stuffing shotguns shells in my pants and shirt pockets. I finally jumped up with my pockets full and three shotgun shells in each hand. When I reached the pasture fence there was no time to go through the gate or step through the fence. I hit the ground and rolled underneath the barbed wire.

That's when I heard the first shotgun blast.

Seconds later came the second blast. That was his last shell.

Down the slight slope I was running faster than I'd ever run before. I felt that my feet wouldn't be able to keep up with my speed but I had to keep from falling because I had the shells!

I jumped over a terrace and there was the battle – my dad, Jip, Sunshine, the colt, and eight wild dogs.

Jip was still in a tussle with the first dog and Sunshine was on the attack. She was pawing, stomping, and kicking at every dog in sight trying to protect her baby.

I could see the blood running down her poor baby's back legs. He could barely move. The wild dogs had immobilized him in a gruesome way. They had hamstringed him. To bring down an animal, wild dogs will take bites out of the back leg muscles so their victim can't run or fight.

"Stay back!" In the middle of it all was my dad. Holding the shotgun by the barrel, he swung it like a battleax. His arms looked as big as a tree trunk as he knocked dogs left and right.

Jip sent his dog scurrying away and jumped on another.

One of Sunshine's kicks landed a solid blow and sent that dog hurdling and whimpering to the sidelines.

The wild dogs finally had enough. They took off running, except for the two my dad had shot and killed. Several of the others were limping as they scrambled to get away.

The stock of my dad's shotgun was broken from the fight. He later taped it back together with electrical tape. I still have the gun, tape and all.

Sunshine was uninjured and the colt recovered remarkably well. Jip came out unscathed too.

Overall, it was a good battle, better than the one my dad lost to my mom later.

"How could you tell that boy to bring the shotgun shells? He's only six and those were wild dogs! You put him right in the middle of that ruckus." My mom shouted at my dad. He really didn't have a good answer. He needed shotguns shells and I was just there.

Jip was getting old though. He was already grey around his nose and mouth. He was also moving slower and didn't seem to be as alert as he used to be.

One day my dad put a scarecrow in the garden and put his old clothes and hat on it. Jip followed him out to the garden and dozed off while my dad was working. My dad was gone when he woke up but Jip spent the rest of the day lying beside the scarecrow. My dad said it was because Jip's eyes weren't so good anymore. He smelled my dad on the scarecrow clothes and thought he was still there. My dad finally had to go out to the garden to get Jip or he would have stayed there all night.

Just a few days later, my dad went to feed the horses and Jip didn't jump up as usual. My dad whistled and Jip raised his head a little and let it fall back down.

My dad stopped, walked over to Jip, and sat down on the ground beside him. He rubbed the old dog on his head and scratched his ears. Jip rolled over a little bit and when my dad rubbed his big chest, Jip weakly played with his hand almost like a puppy. He held my dad's hand between his paws and did a slow playful bite.

That only lasted a few seconds and then Jip laid back down with his head in my dad's lap. Shortly after that he was gone.

My dad sat there for a while and stroked Jip's head. He then stood up, picked up Jip, and carried him to the back part of the garden. He buried Jip there.

Before he left, he went over, got the scarecrow, and planted it in the ground beside Jip.

When he came back to the house, my mom gave my dad a big hug.

"Jip never liked to be alone." I never heard my dad mention Jip after that.

Coke and Orange Crackers

When we rode horses at night, we would sometimes come across country stores that were still open. We couldn't all go inside since someone had to stay with the horses. We usually had at least one horse of questionable stability. My favorite snack while on horseback was a can of Coca-Cola and a pack of orange colored crackers (cheese and peanut butter). The little bottles of Coke were the best but they are impractical on horseback. If the horse stumbled or jumped while you were drinking from a bottle, you could chip a tooth.

Get a Coca-Cola – the real thing
Get a pack of Lance's Orange Colored Crackers (Cheese and Peanut Butter Crackers)

Eat half a cracker and take a swig of Coca-Cola. Enjoy.

Birding

One bright and sunny spring day when I was about twelve, I took a shortcut through old Late Billings' place. I was on my way to the watershed lake to go fishing. Late didn't mind me cutting through his place as long as I stopped for a few minutes to talk.

Now, Late was a twin. His brother's name was Early. Early was the first-born – hence their respective names. Age wise, they were probably in their 60's but it was difficult to tell. They could have been in their 70's but I doubt their 80's. They just never seemed to age.

Early and Late were as different as two people could be, not physically, but more from a motivation perspective. Early held a regular and respectable job for more than thirty years, and he had a side job. He volunteered to help with any kind of charity event. If anyone needed help, they knew could call on Early. Even when he spoke, he had a clear deep voice that added authority to anything he said.

On the other hand, Late seemed more content to sit on his porch and wave at people as they drove by his house. Since only two or three cars went by a day, that left him plenty of time for napping and nipping. His nip of preference was MD 20/20. He called it Mad Dog. He said that if he drank enough Mad Dog then he could climb a tree backwards. I really wanted to see that.

Late also took a more relaxed approach to talking. He really did not put much effort into enunciation so he mumbled – and he rambled. So, he had a mumbling and rambling sort of style that carried over into everything he did.

I had spent enough time with him that I understood most of what he said and could then piece together the rest. It helped that he put emotion into it. It was easy to tell if he was excited, sad, or mad about what he was saying. He mixed in a lot of little laughs and snorts along the way. He had an unusual way of looking at things and he would make himself snicker.

On this particular spring day, Late was sitting on the steps of his back porch and he was holding a fishing rod. It looked to me like he was getting ready to go fishing. For a moment, I regretted having taken the shortcut since I thought Late would want to go with me. Now, I liked Late but when he fished, he nipped at the Mad Dog more than usual which made the Mad Dog nip back more than usual – it was a vicious circle.

It made his speech even less coherent. I did not relish an afternoon of listening to a filibuster of mumbled words with occasional hoots and hollers. Sure, it was fun for the first hour or two, but then he just started repeating himself.

However, what Late did next with his fishing gear changed my life. Late cast his bait towards a group of hens that were scratching around. The hens were pecking around at whatever their chicken eyes could see. One of the chickens finally spied the bait, which was a kernel of corn, and gobbled it up.

Late quickly reeled up the slack in his line. When the hen felt the tug on the kernel of corn, the fight began. The hen started jumping up and down, leaping and jumping. Late caught a good six-pounder and she was putting up a whale of a fight.

Late fought and played the hen to keep it from breaking his line. Sometimes the hen made a run for it and made the drag on the fishing reel sing as the line pulled from the reel. Late was patient. He worked the hen and fought her for quite a while until she jumped into the air and spit out the kernel of corn.

I heard Late muttering a few cuss words in his mumbling tone as he reeled in his line. He checked his bait before making another cast.

I walked down the path a little ways farther so Late could see me. When he did, he smiled, waved his hand, and motioned for me to come over.

"What are you doing, Late?" I could barely contain my curiosity.

"I'm fishing for chickens." I had never heard those particular words put together like that before. However, they rolled easily off his tongue.

"Have a seat and I'll show you. It came to me last night." Late reeled his line back in.

"We go fishing for fish all the time. Why don't we ever go fishing for birds?" He said it like that question explained it all and, to a great degree, it did.

Late showed me how he tied the kernel of corn to the line. He didn't use a hook. Besides being messy when he caught a chicken, he also couldn't get the corn to stay on the hook.

"Cast it out there close to the chickens. One will find it soon enough." He finished tying the corn bait to my line.

I made my cast and waited. It wasn't long before the same hen that Late had just caught came over and gobbled up my corn.

"They don't have much of a memory," Late explained.

Now I have done a lot of fishing, but I had never seen a fish fight like that chicken was fighting! I reeled her in and she took off running again. I tightened down the drag until I could hear the fishing line sing from the strain. She finally took another leap into the air and spit out the corn.

The chicken might have been caught, but I was hooked!

We spent all afternoon fishing for chickens. We discussed techniques and possibilities. We didn't know it at the time but we were pioneering a new sport – laying the foundation. Even though there would only be a few of us ever involved, we were pioneers!

"We need to think of a name to call what we're doing. Fishing for Chickens is just too long." I was reeling in a small fryer.

"Well, when we catch fish, we say we're fishing. Why don't we say we're 'Chickening'?" Late was in the middle of a thought process so I just kept quiet. Inside, I didn't care too much for Chickening.

"Birding! When we catch fish, we're fishing. When we catch birds, we're Birding! After all, a chicken ain't nothing but a bird – it's got wings." Late nailed it. Birding made so much sense.

I had trouble sleeping that night. Thoughts of birding were running through my head. *Birding.* We could catch all kinds of birds. The possibilities seemed endless!

 I ran over to Late's place early the next day. I brought some birding tackle and bait. I had kernels of corn in various sizes. Since we fed the horses corn, I had a huge choice. I drilled small holes in the kernels of corn. It was tedious work but it made tying the kernel to the line much faster and easier.

I also dug up some earthworms. I wanted to experiment with smaller birds.

Late was also prepared. He had a couple of fresh bottles of Mad Dog. I don't think it was enough to make him climb a tree backwards though. That would make birding a little more difficult.

We made a few practice casts with the new corn bait with the holes drilled in them. They worked perfectly. We could tie on a kernel in just a few seconds and it looked much more natural than being tied up like a Christmas present.

"That's a hole in one!" Late gave his approval of the new corn bait as he was trying to reel in a big rooster.

So, that's what we named the bait: "Hole in One".

We prepared for the next challenge – the worms.

We tied a worm onto the line, but without drilling a hole like the corn. Smaller birds, like robins or sparrows, were our target prey. This required a different approach. When we cast out a worm, it initially startled the birds and they would fly away. We had to wait several minutes until they returned. We could then finesse the worm ever so slightly to attract the birds.

We caught a few of the birds but they did not put up a remarkable fight like the chickens. They did add the element of flight, but they were so small that it did not matter much. It was like trying to catch minnows. There just wasn't a lot of excitement to it.

Our next target was pigeons.

Like all the barns in the areas, there were a lot of pigeons living in Late's barn. The pigeons invaded a few years before and they multiplied like crazy – made a mess everywhere they went.

For pigeons, we chose the smaller Hole in One kernels. We found that with pigeons we needed to do a little chumming. For chum, we threw out a hand full of corn and then cast our Hole in One into the middle of the chum.

This was more exciting birding!

Pigeons are fast and worked as a team. When one gobbled up a Hole in One and took off, its wings flapped so fast that they made a squeaking sound. In response to one pigeon taking off in fright, all the pigeons take off in fright. We could feel the wind from their wild flapping. The noise of all the squeaking wings beat against our eardrums.

I'd have a wild pigeon on the end of my line, me trying to reel it in and it trying to avoid getting snared up in the other escaping pigeons. One time both Late and I had a pigeon on the end of our lines. Two at a time! We were having a blast.

We spent the rest of the day birding. I had some sausage and biscuits left over from breakfast so we ate them for lunch. Late spent a good bit of his time nipping and napping but he still put in a good day of birding.

We also added a new rule to practice catch and release – with the exception of turkey, quail, ducks, and other edible types of birds. Late volunteered to take all these off my hands if I didn't want to fool with cleaning and cooking them. I readily agreed to that. He knew that I couldn't catch, dress, and cook a meal that I was going to eat. Someone else had to do one of the steps.

Birding for eating birds would be a bigger challenge than birding for domestic birds.

"Those birds will take some hunting skills, too. We'd have to find where they feed and time it just right to be there at the same time they are, usually early in the morning. That sounds like a lot of work." Late was not an early riser.

"You know, some fishermen fish for catfish and some for sharks. I think I'm more of a yard-bird type like the catfisher." Late liked to stay close to home.

While Late perfected yard birding, I set out to catch as many different kinds of birds as possible. Occasionally, he and I would get together and discuss our different techniques.

I tried birding for crows, but that proved almost impossible. I even read a book on crow hunting, but crows are smart. They can tell the difference between a man walking and a man walking with a gun (and now a birding rod). They have sentries and call signals to communicate with each other.

I bought a crow call, but it just seemed to make the crows mad. They wouldn't land but they would sit high in the trees and put up quite a fuss.

I read that a caged cat would attract crows. That might have worked except that my cat wouldn't make any noises. She just curled up and went to sleep so the crows never even noticed it. I didn't have the heart to poke her with a stick. She was a good cat.

The only thing I learned from birding for crows was patience.

Next, I tackled buzzards. I thought they would put up a good fight and they did not seem as intelligent as the crows.

What gave me the idea to go birding for buzzards was one day I was driving the tractor home from bush hogging a field and I saw a possum someone had run over. There were a couple of buzzards lurking around. They looked big and strong and not too bright, just my kind of bird.

When I got home, I found some chicken livers in the refrigerator to use as bait and I headed back to the location of the dead possum. I tied a nice sized liver onto my birding line, made a cast over near the dead possum, and then found a place where I could sit back and wait.

While I was getting ready, the buzzards just sat up in the tops of the trees watching me. They are very patient creatures. Once I settled in and got real still, they stopped paying attention to me. They looked at me out of the corner of their eye every now and then but as long as I didn't move, they didn't care. I hoped they weren't thinking I might be their next meal!

After about thirty minutes, they went back to their possum. The bigger buzzard pushed the smaller one away from the meal. That's when the smaller buzzard saw my chicken livers. He jumped on the livers and gobbled them up.

I gave the line a tug and the buzzard took off. Unlike pigeons, his friend didn't care. It is not all-for-one-and-one-for-all with buzzards like it is with pigeons.

To fight the buzzard, I had to jump up. I kept the rod tip up and fought him for a couple of minutes. He had the line stretched to the limit. It was a good fight too, but then he just gave up.

He landed on the ground and started jumping up and down as if he was having a fit. I have often heard reference to a "conniption fit" and when I hear that term now, I think of this buzzard. He jumped and twitched, made gurgling sounds and grunted, and then he pulled his ultimate weapon. That buzzard started vomiting, in every direction, on everything. Even after throwing up the bait, it kept going. In fact, it seemed to have turned on the offensive and was after me.

He splattered me across the chest and even in my hair. It was green and foamy and smelled even worse than the carrion that they ate. I threw down my rod and ran gagging into the brush. Running away didn't help because the stench was on me. I looked back and saw that the buzzard was just sitting on the ground, staring at my stumbling as I tried to get away. It looked like he had a smile on his face.

I took my stinking self over to Late's house to tell him about what had happened.

"Tried to catch a buzzard, huh?" The words were out of his mouth before I could say anything. He kind of chuckled. "I'd recognize that smell anywhere."

Each year my dad took us on vacation in Panama City, Florida. I could not wait to try birding along the coast. Pelicans and gulls will eat almost anything! These were trophy-sized birds!

I went out on the pier and caught a couple of small minnow-type fish, tied one on a line, and went birding. I learned very quickly that some people get really upset when a bird gets caught on a fishing line. I didn't use a hook so all a bird had to do was to spit out the fish.

But, no! I was somehow the bad guy! They were fishing for fish and I was birding for birds. I really didn't see a big difference.

"Why do you object to birding when you are out here fishing? I practice catch and release which is more than some of you are doing!" I tried to reason with them using Late's logic, but to no avail.

People looked at me as if they did not understand a word I was saying.

We went underground with birding after that. There is evidently a thin line between sport and horror.

Birding was mainly for Late and me anyway. It was our sport. We tried to introduce others to birding but they just did not have our passion. They just did not get it like Late and I did.

One day while we were birding for chickens in Late's backyard, Late went in the house to get his Mad Dog. It was getting close to nip-and-nap time for him.

I kept on birding and was just about to get a bite from a Guinea hen when I felt something cold against my cheek.

"I thought you might like something to drink. Got these from the store this morning." What with rambling and mumbling, it took Lake about five minutes to say that so I paraphrased. At some point though, I think he mentioned the Republicans.

Late gave me a cold bottle of Nehi Grape soda. I had never seen Late drink, or even own, a soda of any kind. "Hot coffee in the morning and cold Mad Dog in the afternoon, but I can skip the coffee and the cold." That was Late's motto. I was touched that he bought me a soda.

That summer, I went birding with Late every chance I got. He always kept me a cold Nehi for nip-and-nap time.

Crow Stew

Late was about the only person I knew who had actually eaten much crow. Since Late is, well, late, I had to find a different source for a good recipe.

Having attended several political functions and speeches with my dad, I often heard him say things such as "He's eating crow now!" or, more commonly, "He's gonna have to eat crow on that one!"

Politicians evidently have a taste for Cajun food too, since he often followed up with a resounding "He's crawfishing!" He usually pounded his fist into an open palm when he said that. He said the same sort of things at local semi-pro wrestling events.

With that knowledge in hand, I sought out some politicians for a good crow recipe.

"Have you eaten much crow recently?" I asked a former Georgia State Representative.

"Why! I have an exemplary reputation! My record stands for itself! There's no reason to answer that question."

"I'm only looking for a recipe."

"Well, Sir. Always eat crow with a little humility."

Okay. I don't think I have that particular spice in the kitchen.

I then asked a Georgia State Senator. After all, they are the elite. "Do you eat much crow, Senator?"

Well, I'm telling you, he got all upset. "My record stands for itself! No comment."

"I'm just looking for a recipe. Since crows are free, open season, all the time. A good crow recipe could save Americans hundreds of dollars a year." I was being very practical.

The Senator just looked at me as if I was speaking a foreign language, like logic. That always throws off a politician and I felt bad for it.

"Look. If a family of four replaced just one chicken dinner a week with a good crow stew, they could save more than $275 a year! That's real money." I was being logical but since it involved finance, I said it very slowly for him.

"Do we tax crows?" The Senator asked.

"Well, no. Crows are free." That's a sentence I'd never said before.

The Senator thought for a moment, "I stand by my original statement. No comment."

There you go.

I tried on several occasions to get a good crow stew recipe from these experts. Politicians eat more crow than the rest of us combined, but they just do not want to share.

So, when you have a hankering to eat some crow, you can just forget it because the politicians have that recipe all wrapped up.

About the Author

Chicken Nuggets is Robert Tyson's debut as an author. What began as a re-telling of childhood stories is now captured in a series of short stories. Based on mostly true events, these stories present an interesting view into growing up in the rural South in the 60's. Publication is by Grace Garland Publishing. We cannot wait to see the next set of stories, which are already in the works.

Robert has degrees in both Mathematics and Computer Science from the University of West Georgia in Carrollton, Ga. He is currently owner and lead consultant for Winston Consulting, LLC, providing IT process consulting for various industries. A long time writer of corporate fiction, Robert has several collections of stories and two works of fiction also pending publication.